Animal
Fairy Tales

CONTENTS

Marshall Cavendish

Brer Rabbit and the Tar-Baby

Brer Rabbit could be mighty annoying to his fellow animals. And sometimes, when he had stolen their dinner or made fools of them, they got fearfully angry. Take that day he stole Brer Fox's dinner . . .

Brer Fox swore to be revenged on Brer Rabbit — and to eat him, too. So he found an old sack and some straw, and made a life-size dummy. It had a swede for a head, a turnip for a nose and radishes for its eyes. Then he daubed it all over with tar and dressed it up with a jacket, a straw hat, and gloves on the ends of its straw arms. And he stood it by the side of the road. It was the smartest tar-baby you ever saw.

Brer Fox hid behind the wall, and waited for Brer Rabbit to come loping down the road.

When Brer Rabbit saw the tar-baby, he stopped in his tracks. "Howdy, friend!" he exclaimed. "What brings you to these parts?" But the tar-baby said nothing.

"Good day to you. How are you this fine morning?" asked Brer Rabbit, feeling particularly friendly. But the tar-baby said nothing.

Brer Rabbit gave it a gentle pat round the head . . . and his paw stuck like syrup to a bear! "Let go!" said Brer Rabbit, and gave the tar-baby a push with his other paw. And that paw stuck, too, like treacle to a spoon.

"Take care!" warned Brer Rabbit. "I can kick mighty hard!" But the tar-baby said nothing at all. Brer Rabbit kicked him — first with one foot, then with the other. And pretty soon his two back feet were stuck to the tar-baby like flies to a fly-paper.

"I'm warning you! I'll butt you, and my head's mighty hard!" But the tar-baby said not a word. When Brer Rabbit butted him, his two long ears stuck to the tar like gum to a gum-tree.

"Deaf, are you?" said Brer Rabbit, hopping closer and looking for the tar-baby's ear. "I'll shout!" But even when he shouted, the tar-baby said nothing.

"Now see here, you're not the friendliest body I ever met," said Brer Rabbit, beginning to feel insulted. "Say howdy-do or I'll box your ears." But the tar-baby said not a word.

6

"Aha! Got you!" cried Brer Fox, roaring with laughter as he tumbled out on to the road. He took hold of Brer Rabbit by the scruff of his neck and pulled him off the tar-baby and bundled him into a sack.

"Owowowowo! You're not going to throw me into the briar patch, are you, kind Mr Fox?" shrieked Brer Rabbit.

"I've got something *much* worse in store for you!" chortled Brer Fox. "I'm going to roast you!"

"Oh, that's all right then. So long as you aren't planning to throw me into the briar patch."

"What do you mean, 'that's all right, then?'" demanded Brer Fox. "Maybe I'll roast you on a spit!"

"Fine, fine," said Brer Rabbit, "just so long as you don't throw me into the briar patch."

"You're spoiling my fun," whined Brer Fox. "Why aren't you begging and pleading with me?"

"I am! I am! Please, *please*, PLEASE I beg you — don't throw me into the briar patch."

"Well," said Brer Fox sulkily. "I came here to be revenged on you Brer Rabbit, and revenged I'll be!"

So he tossed Brer Rabbit into the very heart of the briar patch. The briars grew so tall that Brer Rabbit quite disappeared from view.

"Eee! Oooo! Aaww!" came the voice from the briar patch. "Aha-aha-aha-aha-ha-ha!" Brer Rabbit stood up, chewing on a thistle. "Now fancy you not knowing, Brer Fox, that I was born and raised in a briar patch. Oh! but these briars are comfortable against my fur! My, but these thistles are tasty! Care to try one, Brer Fox? No? No, maybe you'd best take that there tar-baby home before it catches out some poor, innocent little old rabbit."

Brer Fox ground his teeth and hopped about and shook his furry fists. "Grrr-ooo-aaah. I-I-I'll get you next time, you tricky, cunning, wicked old rabbit. I'll get you next time!" And he was so angry that he turned round and punched the

tar-baby on the nose with all his might.

And that — as you can imagine — was a *big* mistake! Last time I saw Brer Fox, he was all stuck to the tar-baby, shouting cursing, and tugging, and calling Brer Rabbit all the names under the sun.

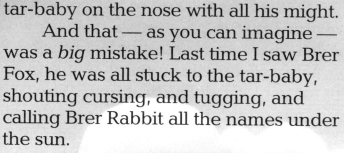

The Billy Goats Gruff

Once upon a time there were three billy goats called Gruff. In the winter they lived in a barn in the valley, but when the spring came they longed to travel up to the mountains to eat the lush sweet grass.

On their way to the mountains the three Billy Goats Gruff had to cross a rushing river. But there was only one bridge across it, made of wooden planks. And underneath the bridge there lived a terrible, ugly, one-eyed troll.

Nobody was allowed to cross the bridge without the troll's permission — and nobody ever got permission. He always ate them up.

The smallest Billy Goat Gruff was first to reach the bridge. Trippity-trop, trippity-trop went his little hooves as he trotted over the wooden planks. Ting-tang, ting-tang went the little bell round his neck.

"Who's that trotting over *my* bridge?" growled the troll from under the planks.

"Billy Goat Gruff," squeaked the smallest goat in his little voice. "I'm only going up to the mountain to eat the sweet spring grass."

"Oh no you're *not*!" said the troll. "I'm going to eat you for breakfast!"

"Oh no, please Mr Troll," pleaded the goat. "I'm only the smallest Billy Goat Gruff. I'm much too tiny for you to eat, and I wouldn't taste very good. Why don't you wait for my brother, the second Billy Goat Gruff? He's much bigger than me and would be much more tasty."

The troll did not want to waste his time on a little goat if there was a bigger and better one to eat. "All right, you can cross my bridge," he grunted. "Go and get fatter on the mountain and I'll eat you on your way back!"

So the smallest Billy Goat Gruff skipped across to the other side.

The troll did not have to wait long for the second Billy Goat Gruff. Clip-clop, clip-clop went his hooves as he clattered over the wooden planks. Ding-dong, ding-dong went the bell round his neck.

"Who's that clattering across *my* bridge?" screamed the troll, suddenly appearing from under the planks.

"Billy Goat Gruff," said the second goat in his middle-sized voice. "I'm going

up to the mountain to eat the lovely spring grass."

"Oh no you're *not*!" said the troll. "I'm going to eat you for breakfast."

"Oh no, please," said the second goat. "I may be bigger than the first Billy Goat Gruff, but I'm much smaller than my brother, the third Billy Goat Gruff. Why don't you wait for him. He would be much more of a meal than me."

The troll was getting very hungry, but he did not want to waste his appetite on a middle-sized goat if there was an even bigger one to come. "All right, you can cross my bridge," he rumbled. "Go and get fatter on the mountain and I'll eat you on your way back!"

So the middle-sized Billy Goat Gruff scampered across to the other side.

The troll did not have to wait long for the third Billy Goat Gruff. Tromp-tramp, tromp-tramp went his great hooves as he stomped across the wooden planks. Bong-bang, bong-bang went the big bell round his neck.

"Who's that stomping over *my* bridge?" roared the troll, resting his chin on his hands.

"Billy Goat Gruff," said the third goat in a deep voice. "I'm going up to the mountain to eat the lush spring grass."

"Oh no you're not," said the troll as he clambered up on to the bridge. "I'm going to eat you for breakfast!"

"That's what *you* think," said the biggest Billy Goat Gruff. Then he lowered his horns, galloped along the bridge and butted the ugly troll. Up, up, up went the troll into the air . . . then down, down, down into the rushing river below. He disappeared below the swirling waters, and was drowned.

"So much for *his* breakfast," thought the biggest Billy Goat Gruff. "Now what about *mine*!" And he walked in triumph over the bridge to join his two brothers on the mountain pastures. From then on anyone could cross the bridge whenever they liked — thanks to the three Billy Goats Gruff.

THE UGLY DUCKLING

It was late Spring, and the sun shone hot on a brown duck beside the farm pond. But she did not stir. She was sitting on her nest of eggs, patiently waiting for them to hatch.

Tip-tap, crick-crack. A pretty little duckling struggled out of its shell. And by midday, five downy ducklings were cheeping around their mother's feet. But the sixth and largest egg was still whole. "It's *very* big," thought the mother duck. "I suppose it will take longer to hatch than the others."

Then, with an enormous crack, the shell broke in two — and out spilled a bundle of scruffy feathers and beak and feet, almost as big as the mother herself. "You can't be one of *mine!*" she quacked, staring at the ugly duckling.

His brothers and sisters all stared, too. "You're not one of us," they said, and began to laugh at the size of his flapping feet. Their father, the drake, paddled across the pond towards his new brood of children.

"Oh dear," said the mother, trying to hide the sixth duckling behind her. "Whatever will he say when he sees *you?*"

The drake beamed at his children and wagged his stumpy tail proudly. "Well done! What a fine family you've given me. Good grief! That's not one of *mine!*"

large, ugly brother. "He's a turkeyling!"

"Of course he isn't!" quacked their mother sharply. "We'll go for a swim on the pond to prove it. Turkeys can't swim."

The ugly duckling was not a turkey. He swam just as well as his brothers and sisters — faster in fact, because his feet were so big. But the farm animals all gathered round the pond and passed rude remarks about mother duck's very *large* child.

The ugly duckling stumbled forwards, with loving flicks of his short wings. But the drake turned his back and waddled off, shaking his head in disgust. The mother spread her wing comfortingly over the ugly duckling, but she could not help wishing he was prettier. "Perhaps you'll be clever," she said. "Your head is big enough, after all."

The farmyard chickens came by to cluck over the duck's new babies. "Oh what little darlings!" they gabbled. "But what's *that*? You've hatched a turkey, my dear. Get rid of it, do-do-dooo!"

"He's a turkey, Mama!" jeered the other ducklings, dancing round their

A tear began to trickle down the ugly duckling's beak and he swam to the far side of the pond, and wished he had never been born at all.

One day the farm children came to feed the ducks on the pond. As they tossed scraps of bread to them huge, long-necked, white birds flew overhead. "Swans! The swans are leaving!" they cried. "Oh, aren't they *beautiful!*" But when they caught sight of the ugly

his shoulders hunched, his head down. He had grown even bigger! At any moment he expected to hear someone say, "What's *that*?" or "There goes the duck's feather duster — that *ugly* son of hers."

Then the same huge, white birds he had seen before, flew over and plunged down on to the river, parting the water with their white breasts. Their beauty was too much for the ugly duckling to bear.

He climbed out of the river and waddled back towards the farm pond.

duckling, the children laughed out loud. "I bet he grows into a whopping great duck and we eat him for Christmas! Let's catch him and show Mum!" And they splashed the water and clutched at the ugly duckling until he was beside himself with terror. He scrambled out of the pond and fled over the fields, to the banks of the wide river.

And there he hid, deep in the reed-beds, day in, day out, although the weather grew colder all the time. At last Spring came. The ugly duckling ventured out on to the flowing river,

As he approached the pond, he saw his brothers and sisters. They were almost fully grown ducks now. They stared in amazement as he passed the farmyard gate. "Mama! Mama!" they quacked, open-beaked.

The mother duck and the drake were tail-up in the water, dabbling for food. The mother lifted her head and a juicy snail dropped from her beak. "Look, father. I do believe it's . . . it's our *ugly son!*"

At that moment the door of the farmhouse burst open and the children rushed out to play. They caught sight of the ugly duckling, stopped and pointed.

"Oh look!" they all cried. "What a *beautiful* swan!"

Reaching the brink of the pond, the duckling looked down at his reflection in the still water. He saw a long, white neck and a delicate white head. "A swan!" he cried, and his voice whistled through his elegant beak. *"I'm a swan!"*

In his surprise and delight he gave one flap of his white wings — and lifted himself into the air to soar and glide, with outstretched neck, towards the river and his own family — the swans. And everyone said he was the most handsome swan of all!

THE THREE LITTLE PIGS

Once upon a time, there were three little pigs who lived together with their mother and father in a little house. But as they grew bigger the house seemed to get smaller and smaller.

"There's just not enough room!" cried their mother one day. "You must go out and make your own way in the world!"

"I'll build a house of my own," declared the first little pig.

"So will I!" said the second.

"I will too!" said the third.

The first little pig built himself a house of straw. The second little pig built himself a house of sticks. And the third little pig built himself a house made of stone. It took much longer to build than the other two, but it was very warm and cosy inside.

Soon after the first little pig had finished his house of straw, there was a knock at the door. "Little pig, little pig, please let me in," said a big black wolf, who was thinking of pork chops for lunch.

"No, not by the hair on my chinny chin chin, I won't let you in," said the first little pig, bolting his straw door.

The wolf growled. *"Then I'll huff and I'll puff and I'll blow your house down!"*

And that's exactly what he did. The straw house blew away like a flimsy haystack, and the first little pig ran squealing to the house of the second little pig.

The wolf came panting after him and arrived at the door of the stick house. "Little pigs, little pigs, oh please let me in," called the wolf through the letterbox, thinking of the nice juicy bacon he would have for tea.

"No, not by the hair on my chinny chin chin, I won't let you it," squealed the second little pig, and he bolted his door of twigs.

"*Then I'll huff and I'll puff and I'll blow your house down!*"

And that's exactly what he did. The house of sticks blew away like a rickety bonfire, and the two little pigs ran away squealing to the stone house of their brother.

The wolf came panting after them and snarled through the letter-box of the third little pig's house. "Little pigs, little pigs, please let me in, cried the wolf, thinking of delicious ham for supper!

"No, not by the hair on my chinny chin chin, I won't let you in," squealed the third little pig, and he bolted the big oak door of his stone house.

The wolf only laughed. *"Then I'll huff and I'll puff and I'll blow your house down!"*

And that's exactly what he tried to do. He huffed and he puffed. And then he puffed and he huffed. But however much he huffed and however much he puffed, not one stone of the house moved.

"I've had enough of this little pig!" growled the hungry wolf. "He thinks he's safe inside his stone house — but there's more than one way of getting indoors."

He fetched a ladder and climbed up on the roof of the stone house. "Three little pigs for dinner," he thought. "Yum, yum, yum." And he began to climb down inside the chimney.

Inside the three little pigs heard the wolf's claws scrabbling on the roof. "Oh! Mercy!" cried the first and second little pigs. "What shall we do?" But the third little pig, who was busy making soup in a cooking pot over the open fire, only fanned the flames and listened to the hot soup bubbling.

The wolf slithered down the chimney and fell — SPLASH! — into the cooking pot. There was one loud screech, and that, I'm glad to say, was the end of the wicked wolf.

The Lobster Quadrille

"Will you walk a little faster?"
    said a whiting to a snail,
"There's a porpoise close behind
    us, and he's treading on my tail.
See how eagerly the lobsters and
    the turtles all advance!
They are waiting on the shingle —
    will you come and join the
    dance?
Will you, won't you, will you,
    won't you, will you join the
    dance?
Will you, won't you, will you,
    won't you, won't you join the
    dance?

"You can really have no notion
    how delightful it will be,
When they take us up and throw
    us, with the lobsters, out to sea!"
But the snail replied, "Too far, too
    far!" and gave a look askance,
·Said he thanked the whiting

kindly, but he would not join
    the dance,
Would not, could not, would not,
    could not, would not join the
    dance,
Would not, could not, would not,
    could not, could not join the
    dance.

"What matters it how far we go?"
    his scaly friend replied.
"There is another shore, you
    know, upon the other side.
The further off from England the
    nearer is to France —
Then turn not pale, beloved snail,
but come and join the dance,
Will you, won't you, will you,
    won't you, will you join the
    dance?
Will you, won't you, will you,
    won't you, won't you join the
    dance?"

The Musicians OF BREMEN

In a small German village near the city of Bremen lived a donkey who worked for a miller. Day after day, year after year, he carried heavy sacks of corn to be ground at the mill. But as the donkey grew older, he could no longer manage the huge sacks and his legs collapsed under him. He was sure that the miller would soon get rid of him — so he decided to run away.

Now the donkey had always liked music, and he thought he could earn his living by playing in a town band. So one sunny morning, he set off down the road towards the great city of Bremen.

He had not gone far when he met a dog lying at the side of the road. "Hello, old dog," he said. "And what's the matter with you?"

"Ooh, I'm too old these days to hunt foxes with the other hounds," panted the dog. "My master is planning to get rid of me, I'm sure, and so I've run away."

"Why don't you come with me to Bremen?" suggested the donkey. "I'm going to join the town band. If I play the drum, you could play the trumpet!"

So the dog agreed and the two of them set off down the road to Bremen.

gate-post, crowing away loudly. "Hello, old cock," said the donkey. "what's the matter with you? It's a bit late in the day for crowing."

"Ooh, I'm old," explained the cock. "I keep oversleeping in the mornings. The farmer is so angry, I'm sure he's planning to get rid of me."

"Why don't you run away with us to Bremen?" replied the donkey. "We're going there to join the town band. I will play the drum, the dog here will play the trumpet, and the cat will play the fiddle. You have a fine voice — why not come and sing with us?"

So the cock agreed, and the four of them set off down the road to Bremen.

Well, it turned out that Bremen was a good deal further than any of them had thought and, as darkness began to fall, there was still no sign of the city.

An hour or so later they saw a cat sitting by the roadside looking very miserable. "Hello, old pussy," said the donkey. "And what's the matter with you?"

"Ooh, I'm getting old," replied the cat. "My teeth are not as sharp as they were, and it's hard for me to catch mice. My mistress is planning to get rid of me, I'm sure, and so I've run away,"

"Why don't you come with us to Bremen?" asked the donkey. "We're going to join the town band. Since you're cat, why don't you come and play the fiddle?"

So the cat agreed, and the three of them set off down the road to Bremen.

A few miles further on, the little group came to a farm-yard. A fine cockerel was sitting on the

" I, I think I'm a bit too old for such adventures," moaned the dog. "And I'm very hungry."

"I'm feeling much more tired than when I was chasing mice," grumbled the cat.

"I'm sure it was warmer in the old farm-yard in the evenings," sighed the cock.

But the donkey said, "Look! There's a farm over there in the woods. If we sneak up quietly, we can snuggle down in the barn, and there may even be some food!"

So the four weary travellers crept up to the farm-house and the donkey peered in through the window.

"What can you see?" hissed the cat.

"There's a table, loaded with food and drink!" whispered the donkey. "But there are three evil-looking men round it. I think they must be robbers!"

The four friends were much too hungry to give up the chance of a meal. So they crouched down out of sight and worked out a plan to frighten the robbers away. Then, very quietly, the donkey stood up with his front hooves on the window sill; the dog leaped on to his back; the cat climbed on to the dog's back, and the cock flew on to the cat's back.

When the donkey waggled his ears, they all began making as much noise as they possibly could.

The donkey brayed, the dog barked, the cat miaowed and the cock crowed — all at the top of their voices. You never heard such a terrible racket!

Then the four friends all toppled over and crashed right through the window into the room. The robbers were so scared they rushed out of the house and disappeared into the woods.

So the donkey, the dog, the cat and the cock sat up at the table and ate an enormous meal. They ate and drank until they were fit to burst — then they put out the light and settled down to sleep. The donkey lay on some straw in the farm-yard, the dog stretched out by the kitchen door, the cock flew on to the chimney pot and the cat curled up by the fire. Tired and full, they were soon all snoring away, and dreaming of life in Bremen.

Meanwhile, the robbers had seen the light go out. "We must have been mad to let ourselves be frightened like that," said their leader. And he ordered one of his men to take a closer look at the farm.

The robber crept up silently and climbed in through the broken window, then slipped into the kitchen to light a candle. He saw the cat's round eyes glowing in the dark, and thinking they were coals burning in the fire, he bent down to light the candle. But when he poked it towards the cat's eye, she leaped up at him, hissing and spitting and scratching his face.

The man backed away in horror — but as he fled through the door the dog jumped up and bit him on the leg. He

hobbled across the yard and the donkey gave him a great kick with his hooves. Then the cock flew down from the chimney-pot and screeched all round his head.

The poor robber had never been so scared in all his life, and he bolted back into the woods.

"Well?" demanded the leader. "What happened?"

"There's . . . there's a witch in

After that terrible night, the robbers never went near the house again. And the four friends decided *they* would never leave it . . . so they never did reach Bremen, or join the town band!

that house! She spat at me and scratched my face with her claws. And there's a dwarf who stabbed me in the leg with a dagger! And in the yard there's a big dark monster who hit me with his club! And a great bat screeched around my ears! I wouldn't go there again if you paid me a thousand gold coins!"

Hare was always laughing at Tortoise for being so slow. "I really can't think why you bother moving at all," he said. "Well," said Tortoise, "I may be slow, but I always get there in the end. I'll tell you what, I'll give you a race."

"You must be joking you silly slow-coach," sneered Hare. "But if you really insist . . ."
So one hot, sunny day, all the animals came to watch the Great Race. Mole lifted the starting flag and said: "Ready, Steady, *Go!*"

Hare raced away, leaving Tortoise coughing in a cloud of dust. Then Tortoise moved off — slowly, very very slowly. Hare was already out of sight.
"It's hopeless," said the Grasshoppers. "What chance does poor Tortoise have?"

"That silly Tortoise," thought Hare, looking back. "He's so slow, I can't lose. Why should I rush? In fact I think I'll just have a little rest . . ." So he lay back in the warm sun and was soon fast asleep, dreaming of cheers and prizes.

All the long morning Tortoise moved slowly, slowly along the route. Most of the animals got so bored they went home. But Tortoise just kept on going. At noon he passed Hare dozing gently by the roadside. He didn't stop to wake him. He just kept going.

Eventually, Hare woke up and stretched his legs. The sun was low in the sky. And looking back down the road, he laughed. "No sign of that silly Tortoise!" With a great leap, he raced off in the direction of the finish line to collect his prize.

But then to his horror who should he see in the distance but that silly Tortoise creeping slowly over the finish line. The flag was down. The Tortoise had won! Even from the top of the hill, Hare could hear the cheering and the clapping.

"It's not fair," whined Hare. "You cheated. Everyone knows I'm much faster than you, you old slow-coach."
"Ah," said Tortoise, looking back over his shoulder. "But I told you, I always get there in the end. Slow and steady, that's me."

The Owl and the Pussy Cat went to sea
In a beautiful pea-green boat.
They took some honey, and plenty of money
Wrapped up in a five-pound note.
The Owl looked up to the stars above,
And sang to a small guitar,
"O lovely Pussy! O Pussy, my love,
What a beautiful Pussy you are,
You are,
You are,
What a beautiful Pussy you are!"

The Owl and the Pussy Cat

Pussy said to the Owl, "You elegant fowl!
How charmingly sweet you sing!
O let us be married! Too long we have tarried,
But what shall we do for a ring?"
They sailed away for a year and a day,
To the land where the Bong-tree grows.
And there in a wood a Piggy-wig stood,
With a ring at the end of his nose,
His nose,
His nose,
With a ring at the end of his nose.

"Dear Pig, are you willing to sell for one shilling
Your ring?" Said the Piggy, "I will."
So they took it away, and were married next day
By the Turkey who lives on the hill.
They dined on mince and slices of quince,
Which they ate with a runcible spoon.
And hand in hand, on the edge of the sand,
They danced by the light of the moon,
The moon,
The moon,
They danced by the light of the moon.

There was once a country mouse who lived in a nest under a hedge. Every day she scuttled about the fields collecting grains of corn. Sometimes, if she was feeling a little braver than usual, she crept into a nearby garden for a tasty treat. Quite often she found bits of cheese rind in the compost heap, or crusts of bread which had been thrown on to the lawn for the birds.

One day she was visited by here cousin the town mouse. "O cousin," she squeaked. "What a lovely surprise. I have such a quiet life here in the country that I always look forward to seeing you again. I could happily listen all day to your stories about life in town. Do sit down and tell me what's been happening."

"Well, I hardly know where to begin," replied the town mouse. "I have so many adventures and eat so many wonderful feasts . . ."

"A feast is exactly what I'm going to give you now," interrupted the country mouse. "I found some very tasty cheese rinds this morning," she said proudly.

The town mouse could hardly believe her ears. She squeaked with laughter as she watched the table being laid.

"My poor cousin," she said. "What a dreary life you must lead. If cheese rinds is the best you can offer, I think I'll go home right now. Why don't you come and stay with me for a while? Everything is so exciting in town."

And, after some thought, the country mouse agreed to go with her.

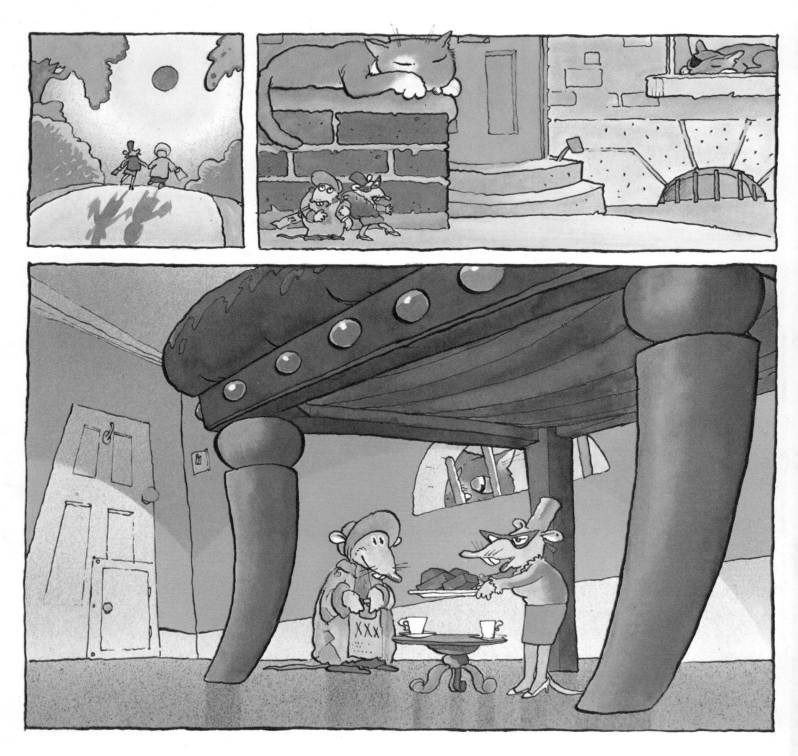

It was a long and frightening journey to the town mouse's home. When they reached the town they kept to the back streets as much as possible, but there were still an awful lot of people around — and even worse, an awful lot of cats.

The poor country mouse was shaking with fear by the time they reached the house where her cousin lived. "I don't think I should have come," she whispered as they tip-toed into the huge kitchen.

"You'll soon change your mind," replied her cousin cheerfully. "Just look what's in here."

The country mouse looked up — and there above her was a table laden with food. It was such a wonderful sight that she immediately forgot all her fears. "I've never seen so many goodies," she sighed happily.